DATE DUE

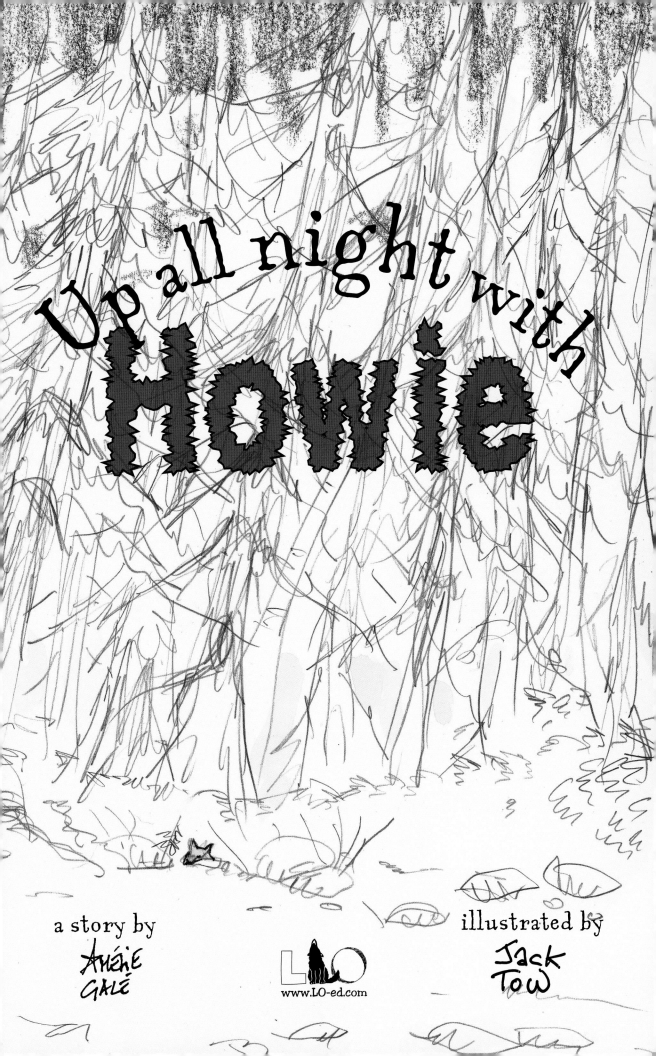

Up all night with Howie

a story by
AMÉLIE
GALÉ

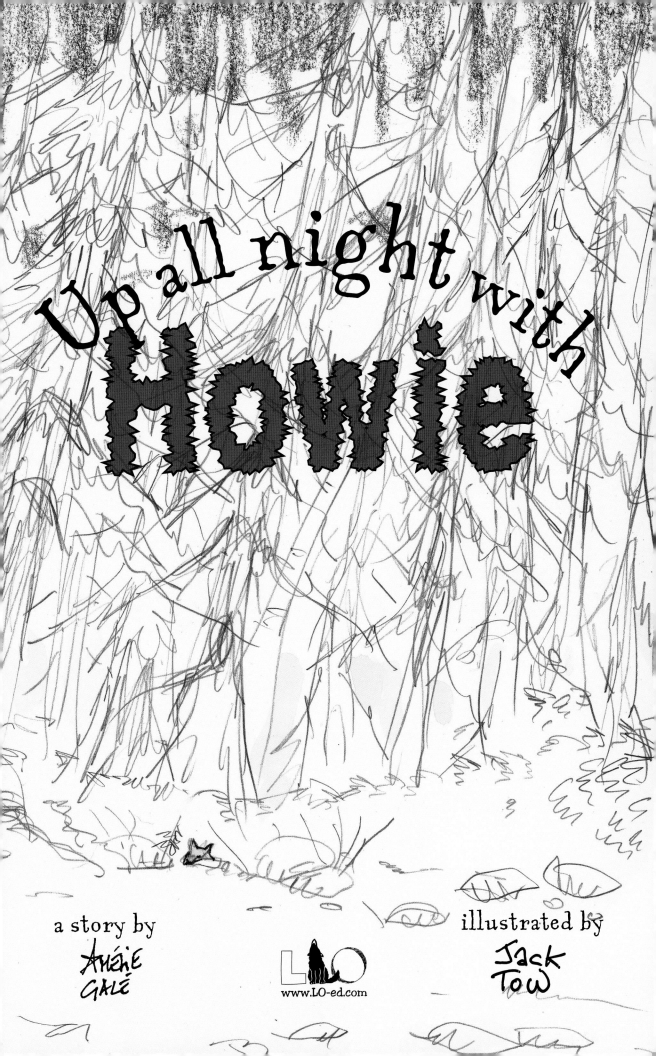
www.LO-ed.com

illustrated by
Jack
Tow

07:30

Hal! Hannah! Are you ready?
It's time to go to school!

Wait! Where's Howie???

This is ME

07:45

Hurry up, or we are
going to be late!

COME ON, Howie,
you are always lagging behind...

Wait up...

08:30... at school

2 black sheep
+ 2 white sheep
= ?

The teacher,
Mr. Lupus,
is showing
the little wolves
how to add

10:00

How boring...

11:00

I'm sleepy...

From 14:00 onwards...

Wrestling
in the leaves

Hal & Hannah's

Biting
& licking

Racing

fternoon activities

A spraying contest!

From 14:00 onwards, not far away

Curling up into a
ball and... sleeping

Howie's

Curling up with a log
and... sleeping

Stretching and... sleeping

afternoon activity

More curling up into
a ball and... sleeping!

19:06
The sunset ends a day full of activities fo

everyone – Well... almost everyone

21:00   It's time for bed...

22:02

What's that over there,
Papa??

Play? Play?
Play, play, play,
play, play, PLAY!!!!

Yes, we are going
to play a new game

...16...17... 23... 35... 58... 62...

...And, quite a few sheep later,

Everyone... really, everyone

LO editions
an imprint of
Officina Libraria
via Carlo Romussi 4
20125 Milan, Italy

www.LO-ed.com
www.officinalibraria.com

ISBN: 978-88-89854-93-8
Translated by Sudha d'Unienville
Designed by Paola Gallerani
Colour separation by Eurofotolit, Cernusco sul Naviglio (Milan),
Printed in the month of August 2012 by Petruzzi Stampa, Città di Castello (Perugia), Italy